NEW   'ONS

NEW ADMISSIONS

*Tales of life, death & love
in the time of lockdown*

Mira Harrison

CP BOOKS

A catalogue record for this book is available from The National Library of New Zealand

ISBN 978-0-9951433-1-9 (Paperback)
ISBN 978-0-9951433-2-6 (Kindle)

CP BOOKS

Published by Copy Press Books, Nelson, New Zealand 2020
Copy Press Books, 141 Pascoe Street, Nelson, New Zealand

© Copyright Mira Harrison, 2020

The right of Mira Harrison to be identified as the author of this work in terms of section 96 of the Copyright Act 1994 is hereby asserted.

All rights reserved.

Except for the purpose of fair reviewing, no part of this publication may be reproduced or transmitted in any form or by any means, electronic or mechanical, including photocopying, recording or any information storage and retrieval system, without prior written permission from the publisher.

Printed by The Copy Press, Nelson, New Zealand.
www.copypress.co.nz

*Dedicated to my colleagues and
healthcare workers worldwide
who have given so much during
the COVID-19 pandemic*

"It was the time when they loved each other best, without hurry or excess, when both were most conscious of and grateful for their incredible victories over adversity."

GABRIEL GARCÍA MÁRQUEZ,
LOVE IN THE TIME OF CHOLERA

ABOUT *ADMISSIONS*

Mira Harrison is also the author of *Admissions*, selected as one of "7 powerful books that bring the UN's sustainability goals to life" (**Charlotte Edmond**, *Big Think*, February 2020).

"I loved the stories, the dialogue, and especially the way each voice rang so true." **Ruth Arnison QSM**, Founder of Poems in the Waiting Room.

"Admissions reminds us of the dramas, losses, triumphs and romances that are quietly playing out every day in wards and consultation rooms all over the world." **Rebecca Smith**, author of *The Jane Austen Writers' Club* (Bloomsbury, 2016).

"If you've ever been a Night Nurse, these tales will drag up sounds and odours from your past that you thought had gone forever! Mira Harrison's painting of her characters at times left me with tears on my cheeks." **Reg Bennett**, retired psychiatric nurse.

"Mira brings to this work her astute observational skills and knowledge of our shared and universal experiences, as women and as health professionals. She bears witness to our common humanity, and the particular roles of women within that." **Dr Mavis Duncanson**, *Pulse Magazine*, February 2020.

"I've never read a more accurate and visceral description of hospital work – not just medical and nursing work, but the (also essential) work of receptionists, cleaners and cooks." **Dr Tony Fitchett**, *Otago Daily Times*, July 2019.

Contents

AUTHOR'S NOTE	xiii
My Mistake Mandy and Heart Boy	1
North and South Jazz and Brittany	14
Labours of Love Sarah and Chloe	35
I Won't Let You Down Ava and Sergei	62
ACKNOWLEDGEMENTS	75
ABOUT THE AUTHOR	77

Author's Note

The stories in *New Admissions* take place during 2020, when the people of Aotearoa New Zealand were in lockdown during the global COVID-19 pandemic. These new tales are based on my own experiences, but the settings and characters are fictional. Any resemblance to actual healthcare facilities worldwide is coincidental. While the main characters in this book are products of my imagination, I hope you will recognise them: I hope they speak to you, wherever you are in the world.

New Admissions follows my first collection of stories about women working in a public hospital (*Admissions*, 2018). Each tale reveals a different woman's experience during lockdown: three of the narrators are new, and the other (Sarah, the obstetrician) reappears from *Admissions*. The different voices and perspectives show the diversity of experiences of female healthcare workers in one country during the global pandemic. However, there are universal and unifying themes of caring and responsibility; of passion, joy and hope; of fear, loss and grief – emotions which define our common humanity.

These new tales are about relationships: the bonds of love, beginnings and endings…and all sorts of adventures in between. I encourage you to read them in the order presented. There are chronological developments as the course of lockdown plays out and other progressions become evident too. As in *Admissions*, the hospital links these women and their lives, but some of the characters are outside their usual workplace, as is the case for many of us during the time of COVID.

Mistake

∼ MANDY AND HEART BOY ∼

Once upon a time – a time only weeks ago, but now two lifetimes past – I used to go to the supermarket on Monday afternoons. In the hour between leaving the hospital and picking up the kids from school, I'd buy food to feed my family for the week ahead: meat and two veg for our dinners, boring breakfast staples, lunch box fillers and maybe a treat or two, if our budget allowed.

I don't enjoy going to the supermarket, but it has to be done, doesn't it? Groceries are my responsibility. Craig has to *Work*. This was mansplained to me soon after we married: the relative importance of his employment in a bakery, compared to my roles as nurse, wife and mother. He *provides*. Me? I work at the hospital, look after the kids and do the housework. I shop.

Every Monday, I heave several bags (recyclable, not plastic) of our weekly necessities from the checkout to my car (hybrid, not gas-guzzler), then drive across town to collect the kids from school (co-educational, not private). I take the children home and feed them a snack (healthy, not junk food), unpack the shopping as I supervise their homework while cleaning the house (using eco-products, not budget-chemicals) and preparing the dinner (home-made, not processed).

You get the idea. This is how I manage our life.

I greet Craig on the doorstep (nodding, not kissing) gather the family for our evening meal (around the table, not TV), and when everyone is finished, I wash up the dishes and put the kids to bed.

Do you notice how I use the present tense? My mistake. All that's in the past now.

***

I wasn't expecting anything extraordinary that Monday. I'd spent all day on the ward, so I didn't know it was coming. You might think this sounds ridiculous: how could a nurse not realise what was happening? But in those before-COVID days, Level 3 or 4 meant the floor of the hospital we worked on. We'd heard of the virus, of course – it had been discussed at handover – but none of us expected anything to come of it. Rosie, who does nights on our ward, said she'd heard it was no worse than the flu, that people were over-reacting. Reports from foreign cities, from cruise ships on remote oceans, seemed very far away. That's where we thought it would stay. But thinking back to the day when everything changed, I remember how unfamiliar faces had floated past the nurses' station, hushed conversations with senior staff had taken place behind closed doors in private offices. I am not senior staff; I'm just a nurse who wipes my patients' faces and holds their hands while they die.

It had been a normal day. I'd helped Shona with the drug round, changed some dressings, washed those who couldn't get to the bathroom, taken others to the toilet, cleaned up afterwards. Nursing isn't glamorous, nor heroic, like they make out in those series my mum likes to watch on TV. A lot of it is routine, yet in other ways it's completely unpredictable. I'm not one of those academic types writing a thesis on how patients respond differently to illness, or leading seminars telling other nurses that everyone lying in a hospital bed is vulnerable (do they think we don't know that?). I just want to get on with my job. And I can't predict the future. As Rosie would tell you, we often don't know what's going to happen by the time our shift ends.

Before I left the hospital, I changed into a summer dress. This was also part of my routine: I don't like wearing my uniform in public places, and I remember thinking, there won't be many days left to wear cotton dresses. The autumn nights were closing in, but that Monday was blue-sky sunny and I was wearing new shoes I'd bought at the weekend. My friend Tammy helped me choose them. Tammy is a shopaholic and sometimes I go to the mall with her and buy things I don't need. It's against my eco-principles, but I like going shopping with Tammy. She calls it retail therapy and it does make me feel better; it's an hour or two away from Craig and the kids, a break from clearing up after them. Over lattés at our favourite café, Tammy suggested I wear the sparkly sandals to go clubbing with her. She said she'd take me to a new place over the other side of town. I said I'd need to find a babysitter, but I'd give it a go.

Do you notice how I'm still talking like all the usual

things still happen? Now I wonder if anything normal will ever occur again.

I remember, as I crossed the parking lot to the supermarket, looking down at my toes peeping out from my new footwear; Strawberry Delight nail polish glistening brightly in the afternoon sun, my wispy turquoise dress fluttering around my knees. Everything had colour back then. I looked up as I approached the doors; there was a young man asking if he could tell me about the Heart Foundation. Normally I haven't much time for charity collectors, but there was something appealing about this youth, with his neat goatee and earnest face, so I smiled when I said, "I'm a nurse, lovely boy, I know all about matters of the heart!"

He grinned back, casually flicking strands of long golden hair over one shoulder, "I like your dress, pretty nurse."

I laughed when he said that, and reached into my handbag for a few coins to support his cause. But he wouldn't take my money, said he couldn't take cash anymore. So I breezed into the supermarket, my stockingless legs in their new high-heeled shoes absorbing a young man's gaze.

In *Fruits and Vegetables*, I picked out apples, oranges and bananas for the week ahead. It was noticeably busier than usual (Monday afternoons are normally quiet) and a lot of people seemed to be staring at their phones, but that's nothing new, is it? As I selected pumpkin pieces and spuds, strange conversations started to reach my ears. A man with a shaved head and a trolley full of Budget Cola was telling an elderly lady to go home. I remember noticing how her basket (two carrots and an onion) trembled in her hand as he towered over her, shaking his head, then pushing his trolley away. At that exact moment, Craig texted to say he'd been called to a meeting at Work, so he'd be late home. Craig is employed at a bread factory, baking and packaging loaves. He never goes to meetings. I suspected – even though it was only Monday – he was using it as an excuse to go out drinking with his mates.

I proceeded to Aisle 1, *Wine, Beer and Other Beverages*. I'm methodical about supermarket shopping, navigating up and down each aisle in turn. It's the only way I can do it in half an hour without forgetting anything, although I still miss crucial items. These days, I have only myself to blame. When the kids were smaller, I used to tell Craig grocery shopping was a multi-tasking challenge more complex than the most difficult video game! To stop them from wailing, as they sat side-by-side in the front of the trolley, puffing out inflamed cheeks to scream more loudly, I used to race up and down the aisles at high speed, shouting things like, "Who can see tins of beans? Let's get baked beans for tea!" I told my preschoolers it was our shopping game, and it's a good trick if you're slogging round a supermarket with a baby and a toddler, believe me. The faster you move, the less time they have to notice the products you can't afford (or choose not) to buy them.

It was in *Wine, Beer and Other Beverages* that I started to notice things were not normal. Trolleys clanked against each other, shoppers piling them high with six-packs, twelve-packs, dozens of whites and reds. Suddenly, a smartly dressed woman yelled at her friend, "Buy as much as you can! We'll need it in lockdown!"

That was the first time I heard the word.

Trapped between trolleys, I looked around for signs;

maybe it was *Five-Dollar-Crate-of-Booze* week or an *Everything-Must-Go-Today!* event. I checked my phone for the date. It usually reminds me when it's Valentine's, St Patrick's or Pancake Day. No special date – only a message from Craig, telling me, *We're going up to Level 3*.

I didn't text back. Another habit: I don't message from the supermarket. My Monday routine is all about getting it done. Assorted fruit in season: tick; rice crackers on special: tick; unsalted nuts and other healthy snacks: tick. I don't text family members to ask which brand of muesli to buy each week. Maybe I should. Maybe if I'd messaged Craig back, I would have known more that day.

The smart woman and her friend continued to hiss at each other across the crowded aisle.

"We're going to sit it out at our bach. Dave's loading up the car now!"

"Good idea! Have your hair done before you go! There'll be no hairdressers open for weeks!"

I managed to do a three-point-turn between the hissing women, my apologetic smile met by the narrow eyes of the one planning to run away to her second home. As I manoeuvred my trolley through the crowd, I noticed some people had more than one trolley: tandems of carts full of booze and toilet paper weaved around me. I started thinking about a sci-fi novel I'd read years ago, where the main character didn't realise a cataclysmic event was threatening his world, because he'd been away somewhere, or in a coma, or something like that.

Aisle 2, *Flour, Sugar and Baking Ingredients*, was a wasteland. Large sections of the shelves were completely empty. I don't usually buy sugar – I'm always telling patients how bad it is for them – but the kids had wanted to do some baking, so I had it on my list that day. There was none. No flour or yeast either. Even the more expensive brands had completely sold out. This was weird: people in our neighbourhood are not the baking type. A huge guy with a trolley full of cakes, biscuits and white sugar rolled past me. I thought about taking a photo to show the students at work, or asking him for one of his bags of sugar so my kids could do their baking, but before I could turn my camera on him, he was gone. Aisle 3, *Toilet Paper, Nappies and Sanitary Products*, was virtually empty too. Not a single loo roll in sight! I thought about how the kids used to shout out, "It's not loo paper, Mum, it's poo paper!" when they reached the age when they thought they could embarrass me in public.

I'm not sure why I kept thinking about the kids that day. I'm not usually that sort of mother.

Moving along the aisle, searching for tampons (one packet a month is no longer enough) I found only bulky packets of Own Brand Sanitary Pads. This was depressing. Maybe there was a supply issue affecting paper products and baking ingredients, but I couldn't think of a logical connection. Reaching up for the last packet of incontinence pads (for my mum) I noticed the filthiness of the barren shelves: voids patterned by intricate streaks of grime.

It's odd what you notice when things disappear. Emptiness wasn't something I'd thought about, until then.

I could now see queues at the tills, trains of trolleys and their pushers, back-to-back, stretching into each aisle.

My phone went off again. It was Craig. *Lockdown coming told boss I can stay at Work.*

This time I messaged back. *What's going on??*

He replied immediately. *Must bake bread will live at Work.*

What?? I couldn't text fast enough.

Boys think we should isolate at Work for Lockdown. Won't be coming home.

I stared at my phone.

I didn't think it would happen like this. Craig leaving me, I mean. I always thought there would be some flaming row, or maybe he'd hit me once too often after too many beers, and I'd be the one to chuck him out, saying, "Keep away from the kids, you bastard!"

My mistake. He hadn't even mentioned the kids.

I didn't text him back. I called Tammy instead.

"What the hell is happening?" I asked.

"They've put us up to Level 3. It was announced on TV this afternoon. Level 4 in forty-eight hours. Didn't you see? Where are you, Mandy?"

"At the supermarket. It's weird. Lots of the shelves are empty. People are buying heaps of booze. And toilet paper." My mind was spinning. The packet of Own Brand Sanitary Pads in my hand moved in and out of focus.

"What's Level 4, Tammy? I don't get it."

"Full lockdown. Everything will close. We won't be allowed out, except for essential work. Didn't they tell you at the hospital? Where've you been?"

"I've been at work. On the ward. They were all in meetings." I realise now I must have sounded really vague, or completely stupid, but the truth was, I hadn't been aware.

Most days at work, I'd have a catch-up with Rosie around handover, or I'd stop at Reception and have a chat with Raelene before leaving the hospital, but that Monday I hadn't seen either of them.

I could hear Tammy breathing hard, as if she were rushing somewhere. Inhaling deeply, I said, "Craig's leaving me."

"What?"

"He just texted to say he's staying at Work for the lockdown."

"Why?" Tammy had become monosyllabic.

"They have to bake bread. The guys have decided they'll live at Work."

"What about you and the kids? What about your job? You're frontline!" Tammy was asking too many questions now. It wasn't the place to talk, either. I could see the wife of one of my patients pushing her trolley into Aisle 3, where I still stood alone in the wasteland.

I told Tammy I had to go and stuffed my phone back into my handbag.

"Hello, nurse! What are you doing here?" Mrs. Ferguson pulled up beside me, peering over her glasses into my trolley, lifting her gaze to stare directly at me. Patients never expect to see their nurses in the supermarket; it's like we only exist at the hospital, or maybe they think we live there. Not waiting for me to reply, studying the bare shelves above my head, she continued, "They seem to be all out of inco pads, don't they?"

"Here, have these." I handed her my mum's packet and the Own Brand Sanitary Pads from my sweaty palms. She looked about to decline my offer, but then accepted the products without further comment and glided away. I was glad she left. I wasn't in the mood to talk. I needed time to think.

How could everything change like this, during my Monday afternoon visit to the supermarket? Nothing had seemed amiss as I'd gently flirted with Heart Foundation guy in the autumn sunshine, only twenty minutes ago. Now the atmosphere inside the shop was escalating, like a pot about to boil over: queues of shopping trolleys snaked from the tills; high-pitched screaming of distressed infants mingled with low-grade snarling from aggressive pensioners; a man shouted at a cashier that he wasn't paying for *anything* until he got his fucking cigarettes. I looked towards the row of cashier stations: rivulets of sweat ran down the temples of shop workers trying to appease the churning crowd. I turned away. Trying to focus, I told myself I needed to find something to feed the kids for the rest of the week.

At the end of Aisle 3, I approached the fridges where, usually, hundreds of milk cartons wait for me to choose one of them to take home. The last two containers looked at each other across the chilly shelf. I reached to pick up one of them, but a pair of grasping hands swept in and carried both away. Hot tears welled up in my eyes.

In the weeks that followed, there would be government advice on shopping normally and placating statements that we wouldn't run out of food; rules for social distancing in supermarkets; communities clapping for essential health workers; nurses acclaimed for keeping a prime minister alive. We would become heroes, saviours, the angels they always wanted us to be.

But this was before all that happened. This was the time of panic and greed.

During the seconds when I stood in front of those empty refrigerators, that Monday afternoon before it all began, a horrible thought entered my head: humanity is not worth saving. Does it shock you to hear those words – from a nurse, of all people?

As the uncharitable thought swam around my head, I couldn't help myself: I became angry. I'd spent my life looking after people who now pushed me out of their way. That person who grabbed the milk – maybe I'd cared for her father, or child. Are you thinking back to the days before lockdown? Are you still convinced you needed all the stuff in your trolley, just in case? I thought about Craig and how he always put himself first – his Work, his mates. Would he even bother coming home this evening, before he and the other men hunkered down together, leaving their womenfolk to manage at home? I'd have to explain everything to the kids, calm their fears, keep them fed and safe, maybe for weeks or months on end. Was this what my grandmother did in the Blitz? I thought of all the work that Craig doesn't do, or even see: the childcare and cleaning, cooking and laundry, clearing up mess in our house. Now, I really would be doing it all on my own.

I checked the time on my phone. I had only minutes to live – less than an hour before my life would change forever. Leaving my under-filled trolley staring at the empty milk fridge, I slung my handbag over my shoulder and marched off in the direction of the doors through which I had entered this ante-apocalyptic drama. Striding down Aisle 1,

I plucked a bottle of champagne from the shelf, checking it was the real stuff and not the too-sweet-too-cheap drink that Tammy and I usually have to put up with. I shoved it into my handbag as I texted the kids. *Stuck at supermarket. Will be late for pick-up. Wait at school.*

The sliding doors had closed by the time I reached them; they were stopping any more people from entering the shop. On the other side of the glass, hundreds of angry faces mouthed words I couldn't hear. I caught sight of the youth at the margins of the crowd, his golden hair glinting in the sunlight. It wasn't difficult to get him to notice me; I was the only person going against the flow. And I was wearing my pretty dress. I watched him move in slow-motion towards the doors. A sweating staff member pressed a button which released me through the seething crowd into the blue-sky day and the arms of the boy with an interest in hearts.

Can you imagine what happened next? Would you believe I took his hand and led him to the park near the supermarket, where we lay on our backs drinking champagne straight from the bottle, looking up into the tremulous branches of trees, which dropped their burning leaves over us as we entwined our limbs? Can you picture my fingers in his hair, the sparkly sandals lying beside us on the grass? Would you believe I kissed him hard, as if there were no tomorrow?

***

Believe it, or don't believe it. Everything is different now; everything has shifted. Maybe you will be more open to realising anything can happen, to anyone, anywhere.

When you are admitted to hospital with complications of COVID-19, you might think about this tale I've just told you.

Your nurse may look like me, or the image of me you have in your mind, but I expect she'll look quite different. She'll probably be masked and gowned in full PPE, which I *wasn't* given to wear in those long-ago days before the pandemic reached us.

I didn't know I had caught the virus, you see. When I wiped my patients' faces on the ward, I hadn't realised it was here. I didn't know anything as I left work that day. When I strode out of the supermarket and took heart boy to the park with me, I didn't know I had given him kisses of death.

It was only when we met again, weeks later, when I saw him lying motionless on a trolley in the corridor outside ICU, his golden hair swept away from his beautiful lifeless face, that I realised my mistake.

∿

North and South

~ JAZZ AND BRITTANY ~

Brittany said it was sick that we were now essential workers. Neither of us likes working in the kitchens of this depressing hospital, but it's still sick. Brittany has been here years, since she left school. I started here in February, the week after I started at uni. I haven't told my parents I've got a job. I haven't told them much at all since they kissed me goodbye on Valentine's weekend (my mother pointed that out, not me) in my new college room and flew north, back to Auckland. They were really embarrassing at the induction events, dressed too smartly for average Kiwi parents, trying too hard to be accepted, as usual. My mother wore a selection of her terrible sports-casual outfits – which are not casual at all – and my father wore his dentist-having-a-day-off jacket, but at least he didn't wear a tie. They tried hard to fit in with all the other families desperate for their kids to become doctors. No one admitted to their hopes and dreams, but you could see it in their eyes.

I don't want to become a doctor. Nothing could be further from my real ambitions in life, but I agreed to enrol in the Health Sciences course to please my parents. Brittany told me the university takes millions of dollars from thousands of wannabe doctors and dentists, indoctrinates them in overfilled lecture theatres for a year, then chooses ten per cent of them to fulfil their parents' dreams for another five or six years *and* pay the uni $70,000 for the privilege! I'll do the first year, but it's not the main reason I'm here – I'm not so sad as to only want to make my parents happy; I moved south because I wanted to get away from home. They were keen for me to study in Auckland, but I knew what that would mean: living in their perfect apartment, or within controlling distance, with my parents delivering meals, lectures and other advice to my student flat. Needing to escape the life they had built for me, I chose the university as far away as possible. In Aotearoa, of course. There is *no way* they would have let me leave the country, their own journey to the Land of the Long White Cloud being far too recent to let me escape. So, I came down here and started to plan a convoluted departure from all those expectations.

My parents are dentists, but I haven't told Brittany. Nothing could be more boring, could it? There is *nothing* boring about Brittany. Nothing routine. I realised this the moment I set eyes on her, in the hospital kitchens on my first day. Our supervisor, Claire, led me along the route to my very first paid job (Mum wouldn't let me work while I was at school – I had to study and practice my violin) along corridors away from the wards, up staircases, through sets of double doors, and finally into the steamy, noisy room where Brittany worked. She stood at a huge stainless-steel sink, muscular arms elbow-deep in water, 16 Up Doc Martens firmly planted on the kitchen floor. As she swung around to look at me, sweeping a strand of hair from her face, she took me in.

"This is Jasmine. Show her what to do," Claire instructed Brittany.

"Hey, Jazz!" Brittany flicked water onto the floor in front of me and scowled unpleasantly. Once we became friends, she told me women should not be expected to smile all the time. It's what the patriarchy expected, she said.

"Hi," I replied, smiling politely, as Mum had taught me to when meeting new people. I tried not to stare at the tattoos covering Brittany's hands, arms and neck: inscriptions of words and phrases woven together like a crazy crossword, so dense it was hard to see her skin beneath. *You will be sorry all the rest of your life if you say no.*

Later, I learned the quotations were from Brittany's favourite books.

Only Brittany's face was untouched by the tattooist's hand; only a single silver stud on the left side of her nose distracted from the greenness of her eyes.

"Where are you from?" Brittany asked, as she led me to get changed into the outfits we wear at work. Our uniforms are similar to the scrubs they wear in theatre, but not as sexy.

"Auckland," I said. The answer I always give. It's where I was born and raised.

"Asian invasion!" A guy carrying a massive tray of dirty plates pushed past us, muttering the insult my family had grown used to over the years.

"Shut the fuck up, Hayden!" Brittany roared, so the whole kitchen could hear. Hayden shoved his tray onto one of the tall racks and started to move away, his eyes not meeting

Brittany's stare. Holding my breath, hand over my mouth, I watched as she kicked him, in a wild karate chop move that brought him to his knees. It was impressive, as Hayden's much bigger than she is. But Brittany doesn't care; Brittany is fearless.

On my first day, Brittany explained that Claire is uptight because she hasn't had an orgasm in twenty years. She then proceeded to tell me about the sex lives of everyone who works in our kitchen (including Sharmila the scary Head Chef) how much they were getting, and who with. I didn't have much to contribute to these early conversations. As I listened to her talk – she talked all the time! – I thought about telling her I'd only done it once, with this guy called Johannes, whose name was far more interesting than he was. He went to the boys' school across the road from my girls' school, and we met at the formal at the end of Year 12. It was a disappointing experience; we said little to each other as we fumbled about behind the toilet blocks. I don't remember feeling anything, other than a weird fascination with his genitals. Having no brothers and an extremely private father, it was an inaugural experience in more ways than one. It was brief, too: Johannes' dick disappointed both of us in under five minutes.

Brittany continued on the subject of Claire. "Last year, during a morning tea we had for this girl who was leaving, Claire informed everyone – after the gift-giving, but before the managers left – that she was going to stop wearing underwear."

"Oh," I said, thinking about my mother ironing fourteen pairs of pants for me every week, one for each day and a pair to wear in bed at night. "Did she mean just at work, or all the time?"

"All the time. She said she wanted to feel liberated!" Brittany shook her head in disbelief.

"But wouldn't she get quite cold in the winter?"

Brittany nearly killed herself laughing when I said that. She shook with spasms for at least ten minutes, only pausing to tell me she was going to pee her pants if she didn't stop soon.

It thrilled me that Brittany told me about our workmates' underwear and sex lives in the first days we knew each other. As she instructed me in my new kitchen duties – washing up dishes and cleaning ovens – I realised I'd never met anyone so knowledgeable about life. *Real life*, I mean, not boring academic dentistry life. Brittany didn't ask me any more about myself, only saying she'd never been to Auckland. I didn't have any exciting tales to tell her about my childhood. There wasn't much to say, other than my parents had given me everything they'd thought I'd needed to get me on in life.

During our first week together, Brittany wasn't forthcoming about her own past or passions, until we were in a bar in town, the Friday night before lockdown. The city was humming. As we left the hospital, Brittany shook out her dreadlocks (Sharmila doesn't allow us to have loose hair at work) and said she liked my new boots. She was still wearing her old Docs and had outlined her eyes with a smudgy charcoal pencil for our night out. I'd bought the Gold Crackle 8 Ups that afternoon (Brittany had told me the shops would close soon) and some new jeans too. It felt brilliant to be behind Brittany as she kicked open the bar door.

"Who do you read?" she asked, as she pushed a crazy-coloured cocktail across the table towards me. Asking who, not what, made it a much harder question to answer. Pausing to think, I took in the atmosphere: all the tables were full; people were starting to dance as the Friday night music ramped up into alcohol-heavy air; a guy in a green shirt looked back at me from a group near the bar. I turned my gaze back to Brittany, studying my new friend across the top of the frosted martini glass I held in my hand. She seemed relaxed in this environment, her dreads flowing madly towards the grimy carpet which felt sticky under my new boots.

"I don't get much time for reading, doing Health Sci." It was the first time I'd admitted which course I was studying at uni, and I knew it was a boring answer. Brittany glossed over it and continued to tell me she read *all the time*, mainly fiction, but not always, as there was much to be gained from non-fiction too. She listed name after name of authors I should read, *how* I should read them, where and when I should read them, and how they would change my life. I sipped on the cocktail that was starting to make me feel warm in weird places, and listened carefully. I studied the words on her arms as she spoke. *Nobody teaches life anything.*

After she had finished her second drink, Brittany narrowed her charcoaled eyes at me and asked, "Why are you doing Health Sci, Jazz?"

"I'm not sure."

Brittany looked at me for more.

"Maybe because it's easy." My answer was not the one I'd thought would leave my mouth.

"That's not what I've heard. If it were easy, wouldn't you *all* get into medicine or dentistry at the end of the year?"

"I don't want to be a doctor or a dentist."

And then it was out there, my statement drifting towards the first person to hear my truth.

"Can't you change course?" Brittany said. Funny how she could be so unfazed by the most dramatic declaration I had ever made, to myself or anyone else.

Courage from Brittany welled up inside me, mixing pleasingly with the effects of the cocktail I'd now finished. "Don't worry, I've got a plan. I'm going to deliberately fail the UCAT, so I won't be able to do medicine next year." Maybe it was the cocktail talking, but I meant it. "I'll make sure I get As in all my other papers, so my parents won't suspect a thing."

Brittany seemed impressed, so I continued talking. "I'm doing people a favour by not becoming a doctor, honestly. I'm not very caring, or interested in old people's bowel movements, or their other bodily secretions…"

"There are lots of ways to help people, apart from being a doctor, trust me." Brittany looked thoughtful. "And *please* God, don't become a dentist! I fucking hate dentists! What gives them the right to charge so much for doing so fucking little?" She paused to scowl at me with perfect teeth, before returning to the bar to buy us more drinks. I watched her go, noticing the guy in the green shirt was looking at me again. As she came back to our table, weaving through the cluster of men, Brittany caught one of them staring at her arse.

"Fuck-off, you immature pricks!" she yelled over her shoulder, and I wondered if she was going to do another karate move. I hoped she wouldn't put them off too much. I wanted Mr Green Shirt to keep looking my way.

After the next drink – more courage – I would tell Brittany the other reason I'd come down here to uni: to have sex. Not necessarily with wannabe doctors and dentists, but with more intellectual guys studying the humanities. That was my plan: find a guy called Sebastian, like in *Brideshead Revisited*. Someone studying philosophy, or comparative literature, or something like that.

***

I didn't get to fulfil my sexual ambitions before lockdown. In the early weeks of March, I was still traipsing down the hill to lecture theatres by day and skipping along to the hospital by night. Brittany said I was lucky to get evening shifts, as I could eat my dinner for free in the kitchen. We usually ate together, piling our plates high with hospital food, chatting in low voices, away from the others. I didn't tell Brittany my parents were paying for my meals in college each day.

Every Sunday morning, I called home to report that I was settling in well and studying hard. Sometimes Dad asked if I'd made any friends, or Mum would suggest I make contact with the local Chinese community, but I brushed their suggestions aside, saying I was fine. I declined their request to do a video call, because they didn't know about the piercing Brittany had persuaded me to get. That was also the day I had my hair cut spiky short.

Brittany had told me I looked really sick when I arrived at the hospital.

"Thanks, man," I'd replied, looking round for Claire or Sharmila.

"They're up on the wards, then at a meeting, so you're good."

I decided to risk leaving my new tongue piercing in place. The thought of removing the shiny green spike was too painful. After it was put in, Brittany had suggested I take a selfie – with my tongue thrusting forward in an act of defiance – and send it to my parents, but I thought it was better they didn't know. Mum would not have taken it well.

I was exhilarated by the idea of my new double life: Jasmine, daughter of dentists; Jazz, the defiant domestic – and Brittany's friend.

***

As news of the global pandemic reached the pristine shores of New Zealand, spreading south, so did the racial slurs. Back in Auckland, it had been part of growing up – nasty taunts in the playground, snide remarks in shopping malls on Saturdays. To be honest, I was always surprised when someone commented on my Chinese appearance. I was a Kiwi. Mum didn't get it; she still thought of Beijing as home. Every weekend, my parents still talked to their parents in native tongues I couldn't understand, didn't want to comprehend. I preferred to go to the marae with my friends.

I didn't tell Mum about the insults I'd had flung at me by other students – and even one of our lecturers (more subtle, maybe, but same meaning) – after certain commentators blamed everything about COVID-19 on *The Chinese*. In those early days, you couldn't get away from everyone talking about *The Chinese*. In some ways, it would have been good to discuss it with my folks, but I didn't want them to worry about me.

It was uncomfortable at the hospital too, with Hayden lecturing everyone about Chinese markets, the lack of animal and human rights in China, not to mention how my *countrymen* had actually constructed the virus in government-funded laboratories. He pointed at me with his bony finger, when he said that last thing, about my countrymen.

"She was born in fucking Auckland, Hayden!" Brittany yelled across the kitchen.

It was a pity Sharmila hadn't been there during Hayden's outburst (maybe she would have sacked him) but Brittany was awesome. She didn't kick him this time, but she put him straight on a few facts. I carried on clearing trays, nodding in furious agreement after Brittany cited each piece of evidence against every statement he made. She summarised by telling Hayden – and the whole kitchen staff – that he was a wanker.

During our break, she asked if I'd be upset by Hayden's ignorance. I said no, not really – I didn't take it personally. Brittany told me I should take it *very* personally and sent me a reading list of books dealing with racism, sexism and other types of prejudice.

***

On the Monday Level 3 was announced, the uni told us to go home. Brittany said they didn't want to take responsibility for us. She told me their plan to teach students remotely was to appease agitated parents, who were calling their babies back to their nests. Mine did too, of course, but I refused to go. There was *no way* I was going back to sit in their immaculate apartment, Zooming in from Auckland to lectures on the structure of cells, eating beautifully presented meals prepared by my bored and boring parents! I told them there was the option to stay, to work from my hall of residence, to support my new friends through the pandemic. The part about the option to remain in college wasn't a lie, although most of the Health Sci students in my hall (I'd made no friends) ran home to their mummies and daddies, to be supported from the comfort of their childhood couches.

I considered whether I should feel guilty about the partial truths I'd told my parents. Brittany and I discussed it, as we scraped left-over food from hospital plates into the kitchen bins.

"Guilt is a lifestyle choice, not a fundamental human emotion, Jazz."

"I know," I said, although I hadn't known it before.

"You don't *need* to feel it."

This got me thinking about which emotions were fundamental, which ones we *had* to feel.

"Is hate a fundamental emotion, do you think?" I asked.

"No," Brittany said. "We don't *need* to feel hate. But we have to feel joy and love and passion to be whole human beings."

I wondered about her assertion that everyone needed to feel passionate to be complete, but by the time I could get my thoughts together, Brittany had moved on to another list of essential reading during lockdown, including a novel called *Love in the Time of Cholera* by a South American author I'd never heard of and *The Plague* by Albert Camus, which we'd been told to read at school.

Occasionally, we were asked to push trolleys somewhere around the hospital, or serve in the staff canteen, but only when other kitchen staff were not around. Mostly, Sharmila kept Brittany and me out of sight of the COVID crisis, and this suited us. One night, Claire asked me to take some fruit and other food up to a room outside ICU, for the doctors and nurses on duty. I didn't stay long. The sight of faceless bodies through the small windows in the double doors sent me rushing back to the safety of our kitchen, where Brittany explained things. She said COVID patients were often nursed on their fronts, so their lungs could move more easily; she described breathing techniques which could stop you catching the virus; she gave me detailed accounts of the number of ventilators available in each hospital in our country; she told me about clinical trials underway in China. I didn't question where she learned all she knew. It was probably from all the stuff she read. She told me she studied several medical journals each week – including the *BMJ*, *Lancet* and *New England Journal of Medicine* – and that access to articles on COVID-19 was currently free of charge.

With our arms deep in sudsless water, or scraping layers of congealed grease from the hospital's ventilation system, or as we mopped the cracked Lino floors, Brittany provided me with an alternative education. There were her research findings to discuss – key scientific publications, numbers of new cases in our region, mortality statistics worldwide – and more personal dilemmas to share. As our conversations deepened, we became closer. One evening, I told Brittany about my disastrous attempt at coitus (as they called it in the Health Sci module) with Johannes at the school formal. I confessed I was worried the pandemic would mean I would never have sex again.

"Might be just as well. There's going to be a shortage of condoms, due to factory closures overseas," Brittany informed me.

My heart sank a bit further. "Oh, God! What next? All the guys in my hall have run away home and now the fucking mega-rich pharmaceutical companies can't even produce enough contraceptives to help those of us who don't want to fucking-well over-populate the planet and have some fun!" I felt quite proud of my speech-in-the-style-of-Brittany.

"You don't necessarily need condoms, Jazz." She looked at me, removing her hands from the sink. I pushed my tongue to the roof of my mouth, feeling the spike against my soft palate. Brittany's suggestion didn't fit with the sex education session at school, in which my science teacher had pulled a condom over the entire length of her arm saying, "Don't believe any guy who says it won't fit, ladies!" I was going to tell this anecdote to Brittany, but she was still talking.

"Or even a man. They're of limited use, anyway. Women have far more interesting lives, Jazz."

Moving towards the kitchen doors to see if Claire was about, she reached into her pocket and pulled out her phone.

We were meant to leave them in our lockers, but Brittany never followed the rules. I looked around nervously, as she searched for whatever she was looking for. She handed me her phone, displaying an image of a bright blue penis.

"Dildos!" Brittany announced.

I scrolled through the images of brightly-coloured dicks. So many types. Some used rechargeable batteries, or could be charged through a USB port. Some models had flashing lights, which one customer had reported as distracting, but generally the reviews were good. The product descriptions suggested they were more reliable than Johannes had been.

"I'll help you order one in our break."

"How would I get hold of it?" I asked, wondering if I should have said 'him'.

"They post it to you, in plain packaging. You can get it sent to my address, if you're worried about Mother Theresa." This was how Brittany referred to my college chaplain, who'd given us a lecture on Christian values during the Valentine's weekend inductions.

"Would a vibrator be considered an essential item? Aren't they opening packages at that postal centre in Christchurch, to check what people are having sent to them?"

"It could be worth the risk." Brittany smirked as we wiped down the last of the kitchen surfaces.

***

I continued living in my neat little room on the mostly empty corridors of my college and was allowed out each evening to work at the hospital as an essential worker.

The students who stayed alongside me were stressed their studies were suspended, that their promising medical careers were being put on hold. Some of the girls on my floor kept posting messages on Facebook and Insta. "*They can't take our dreams away!*"

Brittany laughed when I told her about the other girls. She said she'd stopped using Facebook, because it was another way that the capitalist patriarchy controlled women's lives. She also told me to make sure the university refunded the fees for the courses I was missing. But I wasn't worried about the suspension of studying. I wasn't concerned about the virus either. From what Brittany told me, it was mainly killing old people overseas, or in rest homes. In so many ways, my life was just beginning.

One Saturday, as we were nearing the end of lockdown, we finished our kitchen duties early and I was thinking about skiving off. Claire never worked Saturday nights and there was no one else around to dob us in. But Brittany wasn't keen to leave early. She was weirdly honest when it came to her own employment and always worked all of her hours.

"Shall I make us a tea?" I asked.

"Why not?" She stacked the last of the plates back into the massive wall cupboard. We sat down, hot mugs in our hands.

I asked her if she'd ever been in love.

"Yep," she answered, but she looked sad.

I told her I definitely *hadn't* had that experience yet. I wanted to cheer her up, but then felt a pang of worry myself and said, "I wonder how I'll ever know if I've found the right man."

"Or woman."

I raised an eyebrow.

"Or person," Brittany added. "We don't fall in love with a man or a woman, do we? Don't we love a *person*, whatever their gender?"

This got me thinking but, as was often the case, when we got to a certain point in our conversations, I didn't feel I'd lived long enough to be able to answer anything she asked me. I frowned into my tea. Brittany stood up and ruffled my spiky hair.

"Cheer up, chicken, soon be dead!" she laughed. "I've just finished this brilliant book, *Girl, Woman, Other* by the first black woman to win the Booker Prize. She'll explain it all to you. Why don't you drive over to my place tomorrow and collect it?"

I didn't look at her when I said, "I can't drive. I failed my test twice this summer." Frowning some more into my tea, I told Brittany my father had insisted on teaching me, had shouted at me until I cried during my first lesson, then forced me to pull over, so he could take back the wheel – and control over my life.

"You can drive me home," Brittany said. "Tonight."

I was glad she didn't ask for any further details of my failures in my father's eyes, but it must have showed that I was worried about driving, because she grinned and said, "The roads are empty at the moment. Great time to practice! She'll be right!"

Brittany said things like that – those Kiwi expressions that had always confused my immigrant parents. My mother had once asked me, who was this 'she' who would be right? And did it mean 'correct' in this sense, or 'alright', as in okay?

Brittany was right about my driving. We got into her car, parked in the silent street outside the hospital. It was a real wreck, compared to my parents' shiny top-of-the range Lexus. There was a hole in the floor, where the rust had eaten away. As I adjusted the driver's seat and fastened my seatbelt, she wiggled herself into the passenger seat and opened a bag of chips. I looked to her for instructions, as my parents had always given them – ad infinitum! – not letting me pull away until all their checklists had been ticked. Brittany connected her phone to the sound system.

She gave no advice. "You know what to do."

We drove along the empty roads of our city. The pre-pandemic lanes of traffic had evaporated into the clear South Island air, which smelled so much sweeter than Auckland's smog. The absence of other vehicles removed my fears, and – as Brittany had assured me – I was able to drive! We passed a sign saying "THANK YOU ESSENTIAL WORKERS!" and I called out, "That's us!"

Brittany finished her chips, wiped her hands down her jeans and closed her eyes. I shouldn't have been looking at her, but I couldn't help it. Her face was relaxed and calm. She trusted me. My heart beat with the power of one-who-can-be-trusted, and my confidence surged as I continued to drive Brittany around her home town. As Nadia Reid sang and strummed, I opened the car windows, so all the old people behind their closed doors in the locked-down streets could hear our music play.

We drove and drove. It felt easy, almost natural, to be behind the wheel of Brittany's car. I should have asked her for L-plates, should have driven back to college to get my Learner's license in case the police were about, but there was no one around to check my behaviour on the midnight streets. We drove out to the port, and Brittany showed me where the cruise ships used to dock; we took a road up over a steep hill, where we stopped at a small car park with chooks roaming wild, to look out over the serpentine harbour below. We stood on that hill for a long while.

It was a perfect night. Brittany pointed out local landmarks, as if I were a visiting tourist. That was when I decided I was *not* going back to Auckland. I'd visit my parents at Chinese New Year; I wouldn't cut them off – they could come down and see me if they wanted to. But here was where I would be now. Brittany moved behind me, reaching her hands up to my shoulders. She pressed her fingers into my back, gently massaging my spine. I could feel the strength of her hands through my hoodie.

"Driving is about being in control, Jazz," she whispered in my ear. "And to be in control, all you have to do is relax, yeah?"

I hadn't felt this relaxed in my whole life. I was excited, too. So many possibilities seemed to be opening up in front of me. Brittany's fingers sent tingles into my scapulae. I wanted to take one of her digits and speak the words on her arms, as I followed them all the way up to her neck.

Nobody teaches life anything.

"When uni goes back, I'm going to change courses," I declared, into the dark blue night. Brittany sat down at one of the picnic tables to roll herself a joint. She looked up at me, smiling. It was something new, this look – a warmth I hadn't seen in her before. Like she just couldn't stop herself.

"That's sick, Jazz. What are you going to study?"

"I don't know. Environmental Studies or Human Rights or something. Something important, and with interesting people to have discussions with."

"And sex? Will you be looking for physical intimacy with these new friends?" Brittany was still smiling.

"Maybe. Maybe not. I don't want to be in a dependent relationship with anyone right now. And I'm never getting married or having kids. Who on earth would bring new human beings into this shitty fucked-up world? Do you know what I mean?"

"Yeah…" Brittany blew smoke into the cool night air. It smelt intoxicating.

"Can I try it?" I asked her.

"No," she said firmly. "You're driving."

We drove back towards town, around the Octagon with its silenced cafes and bars. Mud Death performed a mind-numbing set from the speakers of Brittany's car. Once we had done a couple of circuits of the city centre, she directed me south. "Let's see the other side," she said. "Where I'm from."

Navigating down long flat roads, past rows of shops and schools long since closed, we reached a house like all the others in this area, shabby and damp. I parked the car outside and stared out of the driver's window. The house looked back at us with sad eyes. Maybe it was looking for its daughter's return.

"They didn't show us this part of town during O week," I said after a while.

"Of course they didn't, sweet Jasmine."

I wondered if she was mocking me.

"The university doesn't want parents to see any further than the glossy Visitor Centre they built for graduation pics and visiting international coach parties."

Then Brittany quoted someone who'd written about the rich living on hills looking out over the sea, while the poor live on the flat and look at each other. I thought about my parents' apartment overlooking the Hauraki Gulf, Mum's cousins in San Francisco. It was probably the same the world over.

"That's depressing," I said, a bit too brightly. I didn't ask if she'd been happy in the miserable-looking house. Was this where she'd starting listening to Mud Death, under that leaky roof? I wanted to ask why she hadn't gone to university to study the writers she knew so well, but the answer was obvious. It was all around us on the streets where we now sat.

I started the engine again.

"Let's go see the Teeth!" I was directing her now. I wanted to take her away, to a part of the city I knew, although I'd only been here ten weeks. One of our welcome tours had included the waterfront, with a stop at the concrete molars built into the harbour's jaw. When our bus had pulled up, my parents had laughed at the dental students brushing the Teeth with brooms they had recently bought from Mitre 10 Mega. Looking back, I think that's when I decided I wasn't going to follow their path. I told Brittany this story as we strolled along, the off-white sculptures inviting us towards them in the darkness.

"I'm glad you're staying." Brittany said, as she leaned against one of the concrete molar roots.

"Me too." I said, looking at her.

Then she kissed me.

And then we drove some more.

∼

Labours of Love

SARAH AND CHLOE

"Which is more challenging, Professor White – being an obstetrician or being a mother?"

The question had been posed during a *Careers for Women in Obstetrics and Gynaecology* event hosted by the Department of Women's and Children's Health at a well-known university in Southern Aotearoa, long before the COVID-19 pandemic put a stop to all gatherings of more than ten people.

Sarah White was chairing the event. She was accustomed to difficult questions from eager students and junior doctors with their whole careers ahead of them.

"Being a mother is definitely more challenging, because no one takes your pager after ten or twelve hours on duty!" Sarah had quipped.

The audience of mainly young women – none of whom looked old enough to be a mother – had laughed politely. She had wanted to add, when she trained, it was more like twenty-four hours on Labour Ward before she was released to the ward or theatre, to do another eight hours work before she went home to sleep. Or *not* sleep, when you had a child at home who hadn't seen you for two days and wanted you to read her a bedtime story. Sarah didn't usually go into the details of trying to be a mother while working hundred-hour weeks at the hospital. Maybe their experiences would be different. Either way, she didn't want to put them off during their first hour in her department.

In an adolescent tantrum, Chloe had yelled at Sarah – in front of a group of other mothers and daughters at the school's drop-off point – "Everything's your fault because you gave birth to me!" before slamming the car door and storming off to her classroom with several other sulky daughters. Sarah had sighed deeply to herself, too exhausted to go after Chloe and challenge her statement, or to drive off aggressively, leaving tyre marks for the other mothers to stare at. By the time her daughter was a teenager, Sarah had learned to calm her reactions whenever insults regarding her parenting abilities were hurled her way. She'd had years to get used to all sorts of comments from all types of people, including her father (backed up by other disapproving relatives), her ex-husband (backed up by his mother), various colleagues (backed up by their wives) and certain friends who believed a mother's place was in the home. Even her own mum had not always been supportive of Sarah's choices.

She didn't tell the students about these battles. She hoped her experience was not going to be the future for other women wanting to be doctors and mothers. Besides, by the time she became Chair of the Department of Obstetrics and Gynaecology, and Chloe was approaching adulthood, Sarah had resolved all of that would be behind her. The trouble was, as the new SARS coronavirus reached the small city at the bottom of Aotearoa where she had raised Chloe, where she still practised as an obstetrician in the public hospital (nothing would persuade Sarah to work at the poshpital on the hill), the challenges of being a doctor and a mother were not in the past.

Chloe was away on her gap year in South America and Sarah's ex-husband had long since remarried an accountant who had given up work to raise their four children in a million-dollar home in Christchurch. Sarah now lived alone in a two-bedroom villa, not far from the hotel where she and Anil had first made love. She and Anil Malik were still close colleagues, friends and lovers, but about a year ago, when Sarah had suggested he move in with her and Chloe, he had turned down her invitation. He had said he wasn't ready to be a father. And he was very busy as Chair of the Department of Anaesthesia, travelling overseas to conferences on a regular basis. So it was easiest to meet for gourmet dinners and sex on the evenings neither of them was on call.

Chloe's decision to leave for Colombia had been heavily influenced by her high school English teacher, an attractive dark-haired hippie-looking woman, who had made a similar journey to study the life and literature of Gabriel José de la Concordia García Márquez while writing her Master's thesis on empowering adolescents through great works of fiction. She had advised Chloe to take Spanish at school, along with English and History; telling Sarah during one parent-teacher evening that Chloe would find herself through literature. Sarah had suspected the hippie teacher wasn't a mother, given her carefully-crafted appearance of bo-ho indifference (including a full set of perfect nails decorating her elegant finger tips) and her complete lack of understanding of the practicalities of raising a child on your own. But the teacher's influence ran deep, and Chloe had left on her voyage of discovery to Latin America as soon as the school bell announced the end of Year 13 in November last year. It was hard to see her go – Sarah had cried in a cubicle in the airport Ladies' for twenty minutes before she could drive back to work. But it was also something of a relief. As she'd reapplied her make-up in the hospital carpark, she felt at least she had got Chloe this far. Now it was up to her.

Sarah missed having Chloe at home, especially over Christmas and the summer school holidays, but their relationship was improved by the geographical distance between them. Chloe WhatsApped Sarah every Sunday morning and they talked far more than they had in the years when Chloe skulked in her room and slammed car doors in Sarah's face. Sarah thought she detected a slight Spanish accent when Chloe related passionate stories about Gabo, now her favourite author. She had visited his house in Cartagena and sent Sarah a copy of *Love in the Time of Cholera*, which she read in bed on evenings she wasn't at the hospital.

One night, Anil noticed the paperback on her bedside table. "Any good?" he had asked, picking it up and flipping it over to read the back cover.

"Interesting," she had replied, quickly taking the book from him before he opened it and found the page where Chloe had written, *To Snozzy, with all my love.*

She hadn't told Anil that Chloe didn't called her Mum. The pet name, invented by her daughter when she had started to talk, was too private to share with a childless man, however close they were in other ways.

***

As Sarah and Chloe navigated their lives under different skies, the global pandemic threatened to throw everything off course. Sarah's days before lockdown in Aotearoa were spent in long inter-departmental meetings, discussing how the hospital and university would cope with the approaching disaster. She was told all routine surgery and clinics in her department would cease.

"What about my gynae patients with menorrhagia?" Sarah asked the Clinical Director, a grey man with a balding head and shiny shoes, whose specialty on the university website was listed as *Administration*.

"Periods don't stop in a pandemic!" she added briskly, not disclosing she'd stolen this statement from a UN Women Instagram post Chloe had sent her. As the Clinical Director looked down at his patent-leather footwear, and an awkward silence spread around the boardroom table, she decided to take another approach: "Unless you are pregnant!"

Or menopausal. But she didn't say that out loud. Privately, she was suffering from the cessation of her own menses, but menopause was an insult she didn't want thrown at her in a professional environment (and they *would* throw it, or stab it into her back in the men's toilets). The truth was, the end of her reproductive life had coincided with Chloe's departure. She hadn't had a good night's sleep in months, as hot flushes raged through her body and soaked the sheets with sweat. She'd wake from dreams of her daughter (or was it herself?) making love to Gabo in a beautiful house beside a tropical sea, throwing off her blankets into the cold New Zealand night.

But here, in the hospital committee room, she chose to keep the subject focused on younger women's suffering. "This brings me to women seeking therapeutic abortion," she said, making eye contact with each person sitting at the table. Sarah had no intention of being intimidated by the smell of masculinity filling the room, as the front row opposite her rounded their shoulders, looking poised to form a scrum – if only the Clinical Director would let them. She sat up straighter in the uncomfortable chair. "How are women meant to access our services? Will GPs still be able to make referrals for terminations in the usual way? Can you provide me with details of how Day Surgery will be operating?"

There were many more questions that the Clinical Director was unable to answer during the hours they spent around the table. Eventually, he informed all the HoDs that routine surgery and clinics would be cancelled when they reached Level 4. The anaesthetists argued for Level 3, to save capacity for worst-case scenarios. Anil wasn't at these preparatory meetings (he was away at a conference in Buenos Aires) but the other gas men looked terrified. One of them started sniffing when asked for the number of ICU beds available. Sarah wondered if he was going to cry. That would be a first at a clinical committee meeting, but these were challenging days. She'd heard some GPs were talking about closing their doors to spend lockdown at their cribs in Central Otago, and one of the oncologists had already left town, saying he wouldn't be able to see patients at the hospital for at least four weeks. Even the poshpital was closing, but as Sarah pointed out, they performed no emergency procedures in normal times, so that in itself wasn't a problem for the obstetrics service.

The atmosphere was tense, as the hospital leaders played passive-aggressive games with each other, discussing how resources would be divided. They infuriated Sarah, the way they talked as if O&G was a minor sub-specialty, rather than one which offered healthcare to more than half the population.

"How will Delivery Suite function if my staff are redeployed to other units during lockdown?" she asked for the third time that day.

She knew her colleagues already described her as 'difficult' when she didn't agree with them, but she had to keep asking.

***

Sarah's lunchtimes were spent on the phone to Chloe, where it was early evening in Bogota. It wasn't always possible to talk. Sometimes she was covering Delivery Unit, or clinic ran over. But as the situation around the world worsened, it became imperative to prioritise mothering duties.

"I think your gap year may have to change its focus," Sarah said, as diplomatically as she could, after Chloe hinted things were looking increasingly uncertain in Colombia. The NGO she was working with had started sending interns home, and cases of COVID-19 were being reported in neighbouring countries.

But Chloe didn't want to leave. She was having the time of her life. "I've never been happier, Snozzy!" she smirked into the screen.

Sarah was trying to hide her phone from the midwife on Delivery Suite, who had just informed her the woman in Room 8 had been pushing for an hour.

"Increase the syntocinon and I'll be there in a sec," Sarah said, looking up from her screen, then redirecting her attention back to her daughter. "I'll have to call you back, Chloe. But *please* look into flights to get home before lockdown. It may not be possible to leave, soon."

Sarah attended the woman in Room 8 (performing a high rotational delivery using Ventouse, rather than Keillands' forceps) thinking about how there was far more control in obstetrics than mothering. A labouring woman with her feet in stirrups couldn't tell you to fuck right off the way your daughter could, if you didn't agree with her choices. And even if a patient did shout abuse at you, she couldn't get up off the delivery table to leave the country, threatening not to come home.

Chloe did come home. Not voluntarily, or willingly, but because she was sent back to Aotearoa by the anxious NGO directors, whom Sarah suspected didn't want to take responsibility for the young workforce who donated their energies – and sometimes their lives – in unpaid internships on foreign shores.

The night before Chloe left Bogota, Sarah tried not to plead. Holding her phone close, she tried not to beg her daughter to return to where Sarah could see she would be safe; she tried not to say she just wanted to hold her little girl in her arms again.

"You sound a bit snuffly, Chloe," she said instead. "Are you okay?"

"Yeah, it's just a cold going around here. Everyone's had it."

Sarah couldn't get those words out of her head during the hours she waited to see Chloe again.

Everyone's had it.

Chloe's plane took off from Bogota. The world clock on Sarah's phone told her when Chloe would be transiting in Santiago. While she delivered other women's children into the world, Sarah thought about the novel coronavirus journeying, too. Why wouldn't it be in Colombia by now? Why *wouldn't* everyone have it?

Once Sarah knew Chloe was on her way home, she phoned Anil. The time difference with Buenos Aires meant she could catch him before he started his conference day, while she got ready for bed.

"Do you think she's lying to me, about being not being sick?" she asked him.

"I've no idea." Anil sounded disinterested and started to talk about how he was planning to stay on in Argentina, to assist and advise, as the pandemic was likely to have far worse effects there, than in New Zealand.

She fought against the selfish urge to ask, *what about me?* She could already imagine how it would be, if Chloe returned home sick: she'd need to look after her daughter, continue caring for her patients, supporting her juniors, teaching the students. In the tender days when their affair began, Anil had helped her with all of that, holding her in his arms and stroking her hair, absorbing the weight of her worries into his body, as they lay naked together in a king-size hotel bed. But once the first passionate weeks of exploration had faded away, he'd decided he couldn't commit. And now, he was far away again.

"Should I wear a mask to the airport?" she asked him before they said goodbye.

"Definitely," Anil replied. "Full PPE if you can get hold of it. And if she seems at all contagious, drive straight home with all the car windows open."

Sarah took Anil's advice and wore scrubs to collect Chloe. The new theatre sister was kinder than Mrs Whippy had been, allowing her to take a hat, mask and gloves from the shelves. Sarah left the hospital by the back door, throwing her coat over her shoulders against the autumn chill. There had just been another announcement about changing levels and the atmosphere at the hospital was uncertain. She'd had to leave her registrar covering their last clinic before lockdown, but she'd promised to phone Mary later, to discuss any issues.

The roads were busy, but the airport was quiet. The few people awaiting the last plane into their city looked apprehensively at Sarah, masked and gloved, pacing up and down, like an expectant mother. The anxieties had been building in her for days: the usual tyrannies of distance; fears of planes falling out of skies with beloved children on board. And these were now layered with so many other worries:

viruses in respiratory tracts, hacking coughs and weakened immune systems unable to defeat COVID-19. What if it was already running amok through her daughter's body?

Chloe strode down the airbridge, weighed down by her huge backpack and massive resentment about being back in her home town.

"You didn't have to pick me up."

Sarah's heart beat uncomfortably in the knowledge she couldn't touch Chloe, or come within two meters of the child she had been longing to see. "How was the trip? How are you feeling?" she asked, as they walked to the car.

There was no response, until Chloe sank into the back seat and started crying, uttering words of woe between convulsions of tears. Sarah couldn't make much of it out, but felt relieved that at least Chloe had respiratory capacity to sob. She handed her a mask and opened the car windows.

Chloe refused to wear it. "Why are you treating me like this? I'm not a child anymore!"

"I'm just taking precautions…"

"You think I've got COVID, don't you?"

"It's possible, isn't it? Have you had a temperature or cough?" Sarah asked quietly.

"No! Of course, I haven't! I wouldn't bring that back here! What sort of person do you think I am?!" Chloe started wailing again, as Sarah imagined droplets of coronavirus floating around the car. Keeping her eyes on the road, she said calmly, "I know you wouldn't deliberately do anything to hurt me, or anyone else, Chloe, but I still think you should get a test." She was careful not to say, *We should get you tested*, or *I want you to be tested*. This needed to be

Chloe's decision, or Sarah might as well drive her daughter straight back to the airport to catch the next flight back to South America.

Chloe didn't answer, so Sarah pulled over, deciding to ask someone else for advice. She tapped in the number of the local Medical Officer, a scary woman called Heather, whom Sarah knew from the time she'd had to report a case of syphilis in one of her pregnant patients.

"She fits the criteria!" Heather declared briskly. "Bring her down to the CBAC immediately!"

"Right now?" Sarah asked. "She's just got off the plane. It was a twenty-four-hour journey from Bogota. She's tired…"

"I'm not tired! I'm fine!" Chloe shouted from the back seat, before crying and coughing some more in a syncopated rhythm. Sarah thought of the Colombian dance tunes Chloe had sent her, only last week. A whole file of thumping, rhythmic dance music, for *the time of her life.*

"Okay. I'll bring her down now." Sarah knew not to argue with Heather. "Where's the testing centre been set up?"

"In the car park between the hospital and the supermarket," Heather barked. "You can fetch your groceries, while we test your daughter."

Sarah followed Heather's advice, remembering she was all out of soy milk for Chloe. She didn't ask if she could hold her hand as the public health team performed the nasopharyngeal swabs. She knew better than try to be there. Her daughter had been back in the country for less than an hour, and this already felt like an uphill struggle.

She queued to enter the supermarket with other mothers who hadn't been well enough prepared for lockdown. Inside, there wasn't much left on the shelves, and Sarah's shopping bag contained much less than they would need if Chloe tested positive. She trudged back to the car just as it started to rain. The dampness of the day seeped into her scrubs. Sarah loaded the bag of groceries into the boot. Chloe emerged from the tent, smiling sweetly at the nurse who said she'd call with the result tomorrow; saying nastily to Sarah, "It felt like they were poking my bloody brains out! I can't believe you made me go through that!"

"I'm sorry," Sarah said. "Let's get you home. I managed to pick up the last carton of soy milk, so I can make you a hot chocolate before you get into bed."

"I don't like Kiwi chocolate anymore. It's disgusting compared to the proper stuff in South America. And it's not fair trade."

***

The public health nurse who phoned with Chloe's result would not speak to Sarah. Chloe stomped off with the receiver. Sarah considered listening through the wall, but knew there was no need to eavesdrop: the test would be positive. Mother's intuition. Or maybe doctor's intuition.

She heated Chloe's milk. She could see it all unfolding, with the foresight an obstetrician has for the management of labour. It was going to be a difficult confinement at home with Chloe. She would need to work out how she could cover her work at the hospital, supervise her juniors, and maintain her research – all while looking after Chloe. There was also her Mum, in a retirement home in town. Sarah would need to keep an eye on her too, during whatever was approaching. The possibility that Sarah might catch COVID herself was an after-thought. Mary had said something about mothers needing to look after themselves too, but she had dismissed her advice and told her registrar she'd be fine.

She poured the milk into a large cup, stirring in the inferior cocoa. Waiting for it to cool a little, she started cleaning. First the microwave, then the counter tops, then all the way around the kitchen with her household spray and sponge, thinking back to Heather's instructional tone: she'd said the virus appeared to be spreading easily through households, especially those where the mother hadn't cleaned thoroughly enough.

The sound of Chloe sobbing drifted down the hallway. Sarah delivered the hot chocolate to her daughter's bedroom door, to hear about the positive test and the number of hate messages Chloe was getting on Facebook, accusing her of bringing COVID to an uninfected country. The virus was spreading, and the bad news was spreading, too.

Later that evening, Sarah phoned Anil.

"Poor Chloe!" he said.

"Can't these idiots understand that someone who's unwell is *vulnerable*? Patients aren't to *blame*, are they?" Sarah needed to rant.

"No, they aren't." Anil's voice was calm.

"And no one seems to be asking who will care for people with COVID in the community, do they?" She paused briefly. "And not only has Chloe been getting hell on social media, but I've been given an earful from Dr Shiny Shoes."

She explained how, when she told the Clinical Director she was bringing Chloe home, his response had been purely pragmatic: it was irresponsible to allow her daughter back into New Zealand, if she had suspected she might have the virus.

"What else was I meant to do?" she asked Anil, worrying his response might be the same Public Health perspective. "She's my child! I just wanted her home."

"You did the right thing."

His voice comforted her as she lay alone on her bed.

"I miss you," she said.

"I miss you, too. But I've work to do here before I can come back." Anil sounded like he was almost enjoying the COVID crisis. He had always thrived on having important work to do. But Sarah didn't want to hear any more about his other priorities tonight. She was grateful when he said, "Tell me more about what's going on in our land of milk and honey. Is it really as well organised as the international news media are reporting?"

"Not really." She told him about the empty supermarket shelves, how her colleagues were reacting to lockdown, confessing her discomfort at how people's behaviour was changing, as their world shifted into a new reality.

"I'm worried people are retreating," she confided. Even her neighbours had become distant: one had commented gruffly that it was a shame Sarah wouldn't be able to help patients at the hospital now, at the time she was needed most. As if everything was her fault!

Anil sighed. "Kiwis always want to be the good people."

"What do you mean?"

"I mean, there's a national feeling of superiority over some things: we live in a beautiful country; we are democratic and honest; we make excellent sauvignon blanc *and* we win the rugby world cup!"

Sarah noticed Anil said *we*, not *you*. Feeling less threatened, she agreed, "Some people are pretty smug. Maybe that's why they think they can blame and shame those of us who don't come up to scratch."

They talked for a while longer, comparing how the Argentine and New Zealand governments were managing the pandemic. Anil said he thought Ashley Bloomfield was doing well.

"Have you seen his following on Facebook?" Sarah told Anil about the young women wearing T-shirts with photos of the Director General of Health across their chests. There were bags too. She told Anil that Ashley had been in her year at med school.

"Aha! Two degrees of separation!"

She smiled at Anil showing off how he 'got' Kiwi culture. "Yep. He emailed me last week to say the MoH was desperately short of epidemiologists and did I know anyone who might help."

There was a micropause before Anil asked, "So you're still in touch?"

"Yes." Sarah's comments were having the desired effect. She added, "Actually, Ashley used to have a bit of a thing for me." She didn't care if it wasn't true – maybe this would help Anil decide if he were ready to commit.

Another pause. She waited for what she hoped was just the right amount of time, before bringing the conversation back to the present situation. "Level 4 starts in exactly one hour's time. Tomorrow we'll be in lockdown. They haven't said for how long."

Anil sounded relieved. "I guess it will depend on how long it takes the team-of-five-million to win the COVID world cup!"

***

The next morning Sarah phoned Delivery Suite and asked to speak to Rachel, the cleaner. The ward clerk was clearly put out by this request, which came amidst numerous other demands coming her way on the first day of lockdown. However, after much tutting and several minutes of whispered voices and shuffling noises, Rachel was on the line – asking about Chloe's symptoms.

"A bit of a cough and some muscle aches, but mostly just crying because she's back home with me."

Rachel laughed. "It's going to be rough, isn't it? I'm trying to persuade our kindy and school that I'm an essential worker."

Sarah chuckled, then got to the point. "The thing is, Rachel, I need some cleaning materials. Apparently, the virus can survive on hard surfaces for up to nine days! Public Health gave Chloe a long list of instructions, but the supermarket was out of virtually everything. Can you help me get hold of some viricidal spray?"

"We've got what you need here. I'll drop some stuff off after work. I'll bring the kids with me."

Later that afternoon, Rachel pulled up outside Sarah's

house. Chloe had locked herself in her bedroom, so Sarah came to the door to pick up the cleaning bottles Rachel had placed on the step. She moved outside to greet Rachel – who stood along the path, two metres away. The neighbour's blinds flickered. Sarah waved at Rachel's kids, as they dragged their sticky fingers down the insides of the car windows.

Rachel and Sarah discussed cleaning techniques for dishes, hard surfaces, soft surfaces, food preparation, kitchens, bathrooms, toilets and laundry.

"It's much easier at the hospital, isn't it?" Sarah reflected, thinking about the strict regimes in theatre, taps designed to be operated with your elbows, and time to wash your hands for five minutes without being interrupted.

"You can say that again! I can't keep anything clean at home for long, with those two." Rachel gesticulated towards her littlies, who were now kissing the rear-view mirror with chocolate-coated lips.

Rachel opened her car door. Out poured operatic voices.

"Puccini – La Bohème!" Rachel sang to Sarah. "RNZ Concert are playing some great stuff this week. I can recommend it as music to clean to!"

The week wore on. Sarah got into her daily routine. She rose at six a.m. and performed the first clean of the day, including the bathroom and kitchen, before Chloe was awake. At seven, she checked on Chloe. Wearing her home PPE (easily washable top and leggings, theatre hat, mask and surgical gloves), she took Chloe's pulse, respiratory rate and temperature and listened to her chest. It wasn't strictly necessary, as she could tell from the end of the bed that her patient wasn't seriously unwell (a trick learned over many years, from the ends of many hospital beds), but it gave her an excuse to touch Chloe.

They didn't talk while Sarah performed her duties; Chloe kept her masked face turned away from her mother. At the end of the examination, Sarah could reassure Chloe that all was well. She removed her gloves, hat and mask on leaving the room (she had placed plastic bags for rubbish at sentinel points around the house) and cleaned her stethoscope with alcohol wipes. She changed her clothes after each examination, placing them in other plastic bags to be taken to the laundry and washed the same day.

At eight, she made breakfast and took it on designated plates to her daughter's room on a designated plastic tray. She didn't stay to eat with Chloe, although some days they had a chat on WhatsApp while they ate their respective breakfasts in separate rooms. Sarah did not allow Chloe in the kitchen. After meals, she collected the tray from outside Chloe's bedroom and washed her dishes separately, wearing gloves. Likewise, with laundry, Sarah followed all the rules on the Public Health instruction sheet, keeping Chloe's clothes, towels and linen apart from her own at all stages in the procedure. When the weather allowed, she dried their laundry outside, on separate lines well away from the neighbour's fence.

All interior hard surfaces, including walls, light switches and door handles were wiped every few hours. Rachel had provided Sarah with two bottles labelled *Hospital Property*: Solution A, a blue disinfectant, was applied first and wiped away with kitchen paper; then came Solution B, a pink viricidal liquid, which was sprayed onto a new disposable cloth and wiped over Solution A. All used kitchen paper was placed in the sentinel plastic bags, which were emptied three times each day.

Sarah performed the ritual calmly and methodically in each room. Chloe lay in bed, listening to pod casts about how the global pandemic was negatively affecting women worldwide.

Every morning, Sarah called Mary and they performed a ward round together. There were no patients on the gynae wards by now, so their round consisted of discussing women on Delivery Suite and outpatients for whom there were ongoing concerns. A woman with gestational diabetes was now past her due date and had reduced fetal movements, but wouldn't come into the hospital to be examined. Mary said she'd tried everything to persuade her but, like other pregnant women in their care, she was scared of catching COVID.

This was unrealistic, given the few patients actually being treated in their hospital.

"The whole place is virtually empty," said Mary. "It's weird. Even Labour Ward is quieter than normal."

"Give me her phone number," Sarah was worried about the patient with decreased fetal movements. "I'll call and try and persuade her to come in. When are you next on Delivery Suite? We should induce her, before we have worse news to deal with."

Sarah phoned their patient between her cleaning duties at home. She explained that if the baby's movements could be felt less than ten times a day, this suggested it was time to deliver. The patient sounded uncertain but agreed to come to the hospital to see Mary for an assessment. Sarah was careful not to say if they waited too long, the baby might die; there was no need for more fear in these frightening times.

Speaking to someone on a professional level was easier than trying to talk to Chloe, who still blamed Sarah for everything that had happened.

"You should be glad it's only a mild case – you're getting better!" Sarah had declared in a moment of optimism earlier that afternoon.

But Chloe had snapped back, "Why are you fussing over me all of the time, then? If I'm healthy, why don't you just leave me alone?"

***

Sarah hadn't been a stay-at-home mother since her maternity leave with Chloe, nineteen years ago. That hadn't been an easy time, but at least her ex-husband had still been on the scene, coming home after his long days at the hospital, taking the screaming baby from her arms for a few minutes, while she went to the toilet, or had a shower.

Now, no one came to visit Sarah and Chloe, other than Rachel who brought groceries every few days and stopped for a chat, while her toddlers waved from the car. One day, after Rachel had driven away, Sarah found a tube of scented hand-cream in the shopping bags, wrapped in a piece of paper on which Rachel had written, *Try this, after cleaning.* Sarah had never felt more grateful for a friend's gift.

Standing alone in the kitchen, looking out at the delicate fronds of the kowhai tree near her window, she opened the tube and squeezed some cream onto her chapped hands. She rubbed it in, inhaling the smell of life before COVID.

The days passed in isolation. As she cleaned, Sarah tuned into RNZ Concert, as per Rachel's recommendation, and even found herself humming along to Beethoven one day, but she soon became irritated by listeners who called in to say they were having a lovely time in lockdown. And her phone was filling with texts and emails from friends and colleagues crooning about how much they were enjoying the peacefulness of their bubble life.

"So much positivity!" Sarah grumbled to Anil when they talked on the phone. He was kind enough, but it was hard not to feel resentful at his absence, when he'd chosen to stay away.

One evening, as she made dinner, Sarah thought about a book Chloe had loved as a child, with a story called *What Do Mothers Do All Day?* They had found the pictures of the multi-tasking animal mother hilarious, giggling together as they cuddled in Chloe's bed. Sarah wondered if they still had the book. It might cheer Chloe up, but it would probably be better to ask to share one of her feminist podcasts.

Most nights, after she had done the final clean of the day, she sank into bed. As she tried to sleep, she could hear Chloe in the room next door, Zooming with friends. Sarah wondered how Jacinda was coping with her toddler, outside the press conferences from the Beehive each day. The PM looked bright enough – but then again, someone was probably helping her with the cleaning. Ashley, on the other hand, looked tired. Maybe he was covering his own domestic responsibilities these days, whatever they were. Sarah rolled over in bed, letting out a long sigh. They hadn't really stayed in touch.

***

More than a week into lockdown, in the middle of a stormy Saturday night, she was woken by Mary. Her registrar's breathlessness informed Sarah it was an obstetric emergency before Mary could speak. Anxiety moved around in Sarah's gut, as she sat up in bed. Even after twenty years in obstetrics, the fear remains: the underlying anxiety which lies dormant and waiting, until the phone rings at two a.m.

"I've got a primip in Room 1 who delivered an hour ago," Mary began. "Post-term, big baby but normal delivery. The midwives have had a bit of trouble with the placenta."

Sarah waited for more details of the trouble.

"It took ages to separate, they said they were pulling on the cord for thirty minutes, but I think it might have been longer." Mary sounded stressed.

"Is it out now?" Sarah started listing possible scenarios in her head.

"Yes, but there's a weird mass protruding from the vagina. I'm not sure what it is."

"What's the blood loss? Is she haemodynamically stable?"

"Only estimated at 350 ml. Pulse and BP are fine at the moment. I've put in a large IV line and called the anaesthetist, but I'm not sure what I'm dealing with, Prof."

Sarah got out of bed, putting her cell on speaker-phone while she got dressed. She pulled on jeans and a shirt before she remembered she couldn't go in.

"Okay Mary, we're going to have to do this remotely. I'll call you back on Doxy.me, so get back to Room 1 and show me what's happening."

The picture from the dimly lit delivery room was grainy. Sarah could hear Mary explaining to the new mother that her consultant was on the phone and needed to take a look. The patient sounded like the woman with gestational diabetes, but there was no time for a catch-up now.

"Get some lights on the situation, Mary!" Sarah yelled into her phone. "I need to see the vagina!"

She could hear a male voice in the background – something about a haggis coming out of there – then other voices, other noises.

Sarah's screen cleared to reveal the diagnosis.

"It's a uterine inversion, Mary." Sarah recognised the protrusion immediately, although she had only seen it once before. She'd been a final year med student, watching in horror as the obstetric registrar had pulled too long and too hard on the umbilical cord, turning another woman's womb inside out. Mr Rawlinson had been called in from home and shown them what to do. He'd even joked how he had dealt with this rare emergency on a railway level crossing back in Ireland. Sarah didn't have Rawly's ability to tell amusing anecdotes as she worked, but she knew what to do.

"We're going to attempt a manual replacement, Mary. I'll talk you through it. Give your phone to someone, turn up the volume and keep me on video. We need to act quickly."

The screen became blurred again, as Mary's phone moved to the end of the patient's bed. Sarah didn't stop instructing. "Put her in lithotomy. Get fifty micrograms of glyceryl trinitrate drawn up to give IV, if manual reduction doesn't work. And start warming up at least three bags of fluid."

Sarah watched as gloved hands moved across the screen.

"It's all about the direction, Mary. Push upwards, along the long axis of the vagina towards the umbilicus. This is Johnson's manoeuvre."

"I'll try to remember that," Mary sighed, as she pressed her fist against the lump. Sarah knew her registrar would never forget this night, whatever the outcome.

"It looks like the uterus has been out for too long," Sarah said, stopping short of telling Mary she could see that plan A had failed. She thought quickly about the next steps. "Is the anaesthetist there yet?"

"Yep. We're all here, Prof." An unfamiliar voice.

Sarah waited for someone to add, *Apart from you*, or make another judgement. None came. Now it was down to her. They were all waiting on her advice.

"Okay, Mary, we are going to perform a hydrostatic reduction. Are her obs still stable?"

Sarah paced up and down her darkened hallway. She could hear a baby screaming. Striding back to the kitchen, she sat down at the table. She propped her phone against a soy milk carton, took a deep breath and steadied herself before she talked Mary through the procedure which would save the new mother's life. She remembered with complete clarity how Mr Rawlinson had instructed the midwives to place the bag of fluid high above the patient's head; how he had shown the registrar how to connect the tubing to a Ventouse cup placed in the vagina; how he'd explained the importance of securing a good seal; how the warm liquid had flowed into their patient's body to re-inflate her uterus, like a child's balloon.

She instructed Mary with an authority she knew was essential at times like these. The pictures on the grainy screen started to improve. Within minutes, Mary confirmed the uterus was resuming its normal shape and returning to the pelvis. Sarah watched as the clinical situation in Room 1 resolved. She could hear Mary's voice changing with relief.

The infant screamed on into the night. Sarah breathed deeply again.

"What's happened? What was all of that?" Chloe whispered from the doorway.

Sarah turned around on her chair. "That was an obstetric emergency. A uterus pulled inside out and now returned. All sorted, thank goodness."

Reassuring noises from the hospital continued to fill the kitchen. Sarah switched her phone to mute and placed it behind the milk carton.

"Can I come in?" Chloe asked.

"Yes, please. I need a hug."

Chloe crept towards Sarah, asking, "What would have happened if you hadn't been there?"

"I'm sure Mary would have found someone else to help, or worked out what to do herself." She put her arm around Chloe's waist.

"Maybe. But you always know what to do, Snozzy."

Sarah pulled her daughter closer, absorbing her smell.

After a few moments, Chloe pulled away and looked at her mother. "What happened to the baby?"

"Can you hear that screaming? That's the sound of a healthy child."

∼

I Won't Let You Down
∽ AVA AND SERGEI ∽

I'm sorry, Sergei, that I didn't come with you. As the paramedics loaded you onto their trolley in our overheated living room, lifting your frail body away from me, I just stood and watched. You would have expected more of me, I know. But by then, your eyes had closed and your face had collapsed into the amorphic folds of those who are nearing death. After they drove away with you, I called Katina but she only said, "There's nothing you can do, Mum."

They were all insistent that I couldn't accompany you to the hospital. You may not have heard the oversimplified words of the ambulance crew, as they explained I might catch the virus. I'm sorry I didn't stand up straighter, Sergei, as you taught me when we first met. You always used to say, "Take no prisoners, Ava!" when I trembled before those case presentations we were required to give, in front of the old men who frightened us. Back then, we-the-young were intimidated by our elders; now they-the-youth speak to us like we are children. The paramedics called you by your Christian name, but I didn't correct them. I should have told them you used to be the most respected surgeon in our hospital, that they should treat you well, or they would have me to deal with! I should have said if I was going to catch the virus, I would have caught it by now, as I've slept by your side all this time.

I started writing this letter the evening they took you away. Our house felt so empty – it was no longer our home, without you. I wandered from room to room, searching for pieces of evidence of our life together. In our bedroom, I picked up your volume of Pushkin's poems (your other nightly companion) and lifted our wedding blanket to my face to inhale your smell. Do you remember how you carried your gift to me in a parcel wrapped in brown paper, tucked under your arm, as we walked from the church to our honeymoon train; how I unfolded it at the Owaka cottage and spread it on our first bed; how you pulled it around me as we lay in front of the fire, on our very first night together, more than half a century ago?

With our blanket around my shoulders, I wandered to the kitchen. The tiles were cold underneath my feet. We didn't want to move to this characterless house on a flat corner section, but Katina persuaded us it would be best for your health. She said we needed a place without stairs, that our old home was too big, now she was gone. You told me we could bring our life here, as I packed up our trinkets and teapots to place on the easy-access shelves. When I reached the bathroom, I looked at myself in the mirror, to check I was still there. A white-haired old woman gazed back at me. I stared into her eyes, looking for you.

Back in our living room, I found my pen and your writing pad and sat down at the desk by the window. I didn't write our address in the top right-hand corner, as you know where we live. To start with, I copied the date from the calendar on the wall, but immediately crossed it out and wrote instead, *In the time of COVID*. I smiled to myself as the ink dried. You would appreciate the reference, I know.

During our last days together, as the fever chilled you and the cough shook your frame, you continued to fill our home with your presence. You still read out loud to me every day, until you had no breath left to speak. I always loved your voice. In our first awkward weeks of medical school, your rich melodic tones rose above the other young men and called out to me. You didn't know you were speaking to me, as you sat at the front of our precipitous lecture theatre, answering every question, running long fingers through your short hair, as I cowered at the back with the only other girl in our class. June said you were a know-it-all and walked away when you approached us to ask me out for tea.

I remember so clearly how you introduced yourself, Sergei. You said your mother had named you after her favourite composer. I felt your name catch in the back of my throat, as I shyly agreed to hear more, the next afternoon at Arthur Barnett's tearoom. Over delicate china cups, you told me the story of your mother's flight from Russia, how she raised you alone in a cold Wellington villa, playing recordings of Rachmaninov on a gramophone she bought with her first pay-cheque, reading you poems at bedtime from the collection of books she had packed in her trunk. You said she always read Pushkin in Russian, as he couldn't be understood in any other language. It all sounded so romantic to me, a girl from the sticks. I'd never been anywhere, until then. As you poured me more tea, I stared at the pretty cakes sitting on lacy doilies between us and didn't eat a thing.

The first night you were gone, I couldn't sleep. I lay in the darkness imagining you were still here, your warmth against me in our bed. I always loved your body, your touch. I remember the first time we were naked together, in the damp cottage in Owaka, where you made love to me on the floor. As we lay on our wedding blanket, in the light of logs burning gently beside us, we discovered each other. Your limbs wrapped around me afterwards, your rough cheek against my face, your tongue absorbing my tears as they rolled from my eyes to your lips. Years later, when you had to go away, you wrote to me. You said it had been your perfect hour, as my body turned to gold and you knew you could never do anything less than love me. I've kept all your letters, in a box under our bed. I adore the way you always sign them with a large curly S, with two small kisses and a hug underneath. *Ex-Ex-Oh!*

No one knows about our life-long correspondence, not even Katina. Especially not Katina. She'll find them soon enough.

In the morning, after I'd made myself a cup of tea, I phoned the ward. They said you'd had a comfortable night. I knew they were lying. The games hospital staff play with relatives! It was all much stricter back in our day – so many rules: *No visiting before noon! No husbands during childbirth! No children allowed on the ward!*

My medical training taught me to be feisty. Once we started seeing patients, I stopped hiding at the back of the student crowd. The first time I held my stethoscope against an old man's chest wall, my other hand gently resting on his shoulder (a trick I learned to stop us both from shaking), I knew I could do it. As you and your rugby-playing mates looked on, I showed you this was something women could do – *should* do. It wasn't easy building confidence in those days, the loud bravado of medical men in my ears. But when I said I wanted to become a surgeon, you became my greatest ally. You said I inspired you, I'd shown you how to break the rules of the game.

I wasn't in the mood for playing their games that morning. I said I needed to see you. The nurse used a certain tone of voice when she explained it was forbidden. You would have recognised it, as I did, Sergei. It was pity. I heard it clinging to her words. Why do they pity us, when they know so little about me and you? We spent our life at the hospital they now claim as their own. Soon, there will be a new one for the next generation to run. They will have their day, as we had ours.

I could feel the nurse wanting me to say, *okeydokey my dear*, like other old women would say, but do they not understand they can never keep us from each other? I told her they couldn't forbid it. I was stronger that time; I challenged her authority. She became quite shirty, saying Jacinda had made it extremely clear. They are taking their orders directly from the Prime Minister now! I have to admit, she is quite convincing on TV every day with that tired-looking man, although she smiles too much. He's serious and boring, she's like a primary school teacher. Katina thinks Ms Ardern is a great example of compassionate female leadership and tells me the whole world should follow her example. I told Katina there is more to being a powerful woman than talking to everyone as if we are children.

For the last two weeks, since the morning I shouted at Jacinda's nurse, Katina has taken to phoning me every day. She insists I use the cell phone she bought me before she moved to Moscow. It's almost five years now since we've seen them – I mean, really *seen* Katina and Mark and our grandchildren, rather than watching them wave to us from the tiny screen in my hand.

Katina phones me every day at five p.m. I suspect the nurse may have tipped our daughter off and told her to keep checking on me. After we have discussed the time difference (we always start with this – it's still morning there, early evening here) and given each other a weather report (it's still end of winter there, end of summer here) Katina gives me one of her little talks on the epidemiology or virology of COVID-19 (I refrain from asking her if these specialist areas were covered in her anthropology degree) and, at the end of her lecture, she reminds me to wash my hands.

"I was a surgeon, Katina! I know how to wash my bloody hands!" I yelled at her one day, when it all became too much. Katina said, *I wish you would call me Kate*. You would have smiled to yourself, had you been able to hear us. After I put the phone down, you would have stroked my shoulders and put the kettle on.

Between the daily calls from our beloved daughter, in the many hours I have to fill here alone in my cell, I think about you, Sergei. I picture you lying between white hospital sheets, surrounded by strangers in their protective layers. Is there a view from your window? Can you see the trees in the hospital garden where we used to walk? I try not to imagine your chest wall heaving up and down, your rasping cough, or the terrifying notion that perhaps you can't breathe. I'm sorry to admit my despair to you, Sergei, but you always said I could. In your very first letter, you asked me to share all my fears with you. Your scruffy note, written after our heart-bleeding honeymoon row, pushed under the bedroom door in the Owaka cottage, was your most passionate epistle. You confessed how our love frightened you in its depth and complexity, how you thought admitting your feelings would make you look weak in my eyes, and this was something you couldn't ever bear. *Ex-Ex-Oh!*

Reading your tenderness, as I sat on the creaky iron bed, I wept. I'd thought that love only frightened women.

I'd opened the bedroom door to find you in the kitchen, making us cups of tea. Smoky aromas of Russian leaves mingled with the tang of lemons you were slicing to accompany your brew. When you turned towards me, your tear-stained face fell into your lop-sided smile. As I crossed the kitchen, your arms opened wide and you pulled me in. I can still feel your breath on my neck, as you held me close.

***

We have been told to stay at home and turn on the TV for daily updates, which I did, for a while. The media men have created their image of the novel coronavirus: a glaring shining crown of many colours, replicating gayly behind the heads of youthful reporters grimacing their way through this crisis. You would have shouted at them that corona means *wreath* in Latin, that the well-groomed politicians should do their *research* before telling us what to do. We would have found our old textbooks and discussed viral pathology late into the night. I should have written to Dr Bloomfield to say they can't hold us prisoners forever, but I doubt he would listen to me. Elderly women are invisible to the young – even those of us who know a thing or two about disease.

After too many doses of their computer-generated facts and figures, I switched off the set and looked out of our window across the deserted street. I haven't seen anyone for days. How I miss all those insignificant interactions we used to take for granted. How I miss you, Sergei. During the hours I wait for someone to walk past our house, loneliness closes in on me. Everyone has disappeared. Where are our neighbours, our friends who used to call? How are they filling these hours behind their four walls? Last week, a young woman from the local church dropped a bag of groceries at the front door, but she wouldn't come in. From behind her mask at the end of our drive, she said brightly, "Stay safe, stay well!" before rushing away in her car. I wanted to challenge her on those instructions – how can I be safe and well, without you? – but as you'll know by now, prisoners don't have the right to object.

I've been an inmate before. Do you remember the night Katina was born, when my blood – her blood! – soaked into the sheets of our hospital flat, how you carried me along the uneven path to Labour Ward and lifted me gently onto the operating table, where you brought her into the world? I feared I was going to die. You wouldn't hear of it. When Matron tried to send you away, you stood tall and said directly to her, "I am not going anywhere, Sister." Through the agony of my antepartum haemorrhage, I told you off for speaking to her like that – but only after she had scurried away to carry out the instructions that would save my life. You saved me, Sergei. After you had delivered our child and placed her in my arms, once you knew the bleeding had stopped and you finally went home to sleep, you wrote to me again. During the weeks I was imprisoned in the maternity hospital learning how to be a mother, your words of love, your joyful descriptions of new fatherhood, helped me through the difficult days of learning to care for our premature infant. You calmed my fears, once more. Your letters looked forward to all our new family would do together, your hopes for our daughter. Our plans to travel to Russia and find your mother's home, our brilliant surgical careers winding far into our futures.

Can it really be more than fifty years since I lay in our hospital, while my placenta – Katina's placenta! – announced its separation from my uterine wall, crimson waters pouring down my legs, threatening to wash away all of our lives? I've been thinking about all the partings we have endured over all these years. Some lasting months, some only minutes. Time is playing strange tricks on me during these never-ending weeks. It's become difficult to distinguish one day from another. As I sit at our window each afternoon, listening to your crackly gramophone play Rachmaninov's last symphonic dances – I agree with you, his final compositions were his most poignant – I've noticed the nights are closing in.

Do you fear death, Sergei? We both know, when the end is

near, calmness descends. Anxiety is no longer the sharpened scalpel-blade of our youth, threatening to cut us apart. We grew to know the joy of parting is to be together again.

After our honeymoon, when you were called to serve our nation, you wrote to me from your tent at Burnham's freezing army camp. You wrote to me of love. You described the despair you felt that night, after our newly-weds' fight at Owaka. You confessed your concern that I would leave you and never come back again.

You wrote to me: *To love is to fear.*

Before you signed your swirling S, before you kissed me goodbye, you said that you couldn't live without me by your side. *Ex-Ex-Oh.*

***

Yesterday, Katina called to tell me you are worse. The doctors on ICU called her, not me. Do they think I can't face what our future holds? You always warned them, I'm stronger than I look! I can't save you Sergei, but I won't let you down.

There was a long silence before Katina asked, "Are you alright, Mum?"

"Of course I'm not!" I shouted feistily into the phone.

I turned it off and put it away in a drawer. Then I sat down at the table to make my plan. I'm not going to document the details in this letter – I am not going to give any of them opportunity to stop me – but you know what I will do. Everything is in my head: the roads to the hospital where you are waiting for me; the routes around the theatres where we operated together; the uneven path to the ward where

Katina was born; the plan of labyrinthine corridors which will bring me to the place where you will die.

Before I leave, I will pack our precious things: I will bring your Pushkin and read his words out loud to you; I'll bring smoky tea to hold to your lips; I will cover you with our wedding blanket. Its softness still smells of us.

You are not going to die alone, Sergei. I will come to you.

∼

Acknowledgements

Many thanks to Ruth Arnison, Craig Arthur, Biz Boyle, Paul Enright, Tanya Findlater, Jane Hall, Jean Harrison, Sarah Harrison, Peter Radue, Matt Saxton, Tharani Sivananthan, George Smerdon, Rebecca Smith, Yolanda van Heezik, Tracy White, Sophia Wilson and Jonathan Woolrych for reading early drafts of some or all of the stories.

Thanks also to Michelle Elvy who edited this volume of tales – I appreciate all you have taught me.

My friends and colleagues in the International Society of Pharmacovigilance (ISoP) might be disappointed I haven't included a story about drug safety in this collection, but I hope you will enjoy this new book from your President. Thanks for your interest in my writing endeavours!

I would also like to acknowledge encouragement from colleagues in the University of Otago Medical Humanities peer group, chaired by Dr Katherine Hall; the Southern Health and Disability Ethics Committee, chaired by Sarah Gunningham; the Ōtepoti City of Literature team, directed by Nicky Page; and my literary agent Tom Cull.

Finally, as always, I am grateful for my whānau's ongoing love and support. Special thanks to Jonny for all the cooking and cleaning and love during lockdown – while caring for patients, too. Thanks to my children Alexander and Katharine Woolrych – and to my Mum, Jean Harrison. It's hard without Dad, but he lives on in us.

About the Author

Mira Harrison is a doctor-turned-writer who has worked in hospitals, universities and government agencies in Aotearoa New Zealand and the United Kingdom. She now lives in Ōtepoti Dunedin, UNESCO City of Literature, with her husband Jonny and Mangu, their cat.

Mira's medical career has encompassed women's health, medicines regulation, drug safety research and medical ethics. She is proud to be the first female President of the International Society of Pharmacovigilance. Mira is also a fellow of the Royal College of Obstetricians and Gynaecologists and a member of a national Health and Disability Ethics Committee.

Writing as Mira Harrison-Woolrych, she has edited two medical textbooks, *Medicines for Women* (Springer International 2015) and *An Introduction to Pharmacovigilance*

(John Wiley and Sons, 2017). Mira's first work of fiction, *Admissions* (Steele Roberts Aotearoa) – a collection of stories about women working in a public hospital – was published in New Zealand in 2018 and became available on Amazon KDP in 2020.

If you enjoyed these stories, follow Mira on Twitter @MiraHarrison4 – where she describes herself as an *advocate for women's health and feminist leadership* – and please leave a review of her books on Amazon, Goodreads, or other literary platforms.

Mira may be contacted via her website: miraharrison.com

AUTHOR PHOTO: JONATHAN WOOLRYCH

Lightning Source UK Ltd.
Milton Keynes UK
UKHW011238311220
376133UK00001B/135